Chloe
the Topaz
Fairy

To Rachel and Anna Prockter,
two fairy friends

Special thanks to
Linda Chapman

No part of this work may be reproduced, stored in a
retrieval system, or transmitted in any form or by any
means, electronic, mechanical, photocopying, recording, or otherwise,
without written permission of the publisher. For information
regarding permission, write to Working Partners Limited,
1 Albion Place, London, W6 0QT, United Kingdom.

ISBN-10: 0-439-93531-8
ISBN-13: 978-0-439-93531-9

12 11 10 9 8 7 6 5 4 3 2   7 8 9 10 11 12/0

Printed in the U.S.A.   40

First Scholastic printing, July 2007

Chloe
the Topaz
Fairy

by Daisy Meadows

illustrated by Georgie Ripper

SCHOLASTIC INC.

New York Toronto London Auckland Sydney
Mexico City New Delhi Hong Kong Buenos Aires

The Fairyland Palace

Adventure Playground

Tippington Manor

Tippington Town

The Tall Toy Store

Fountain

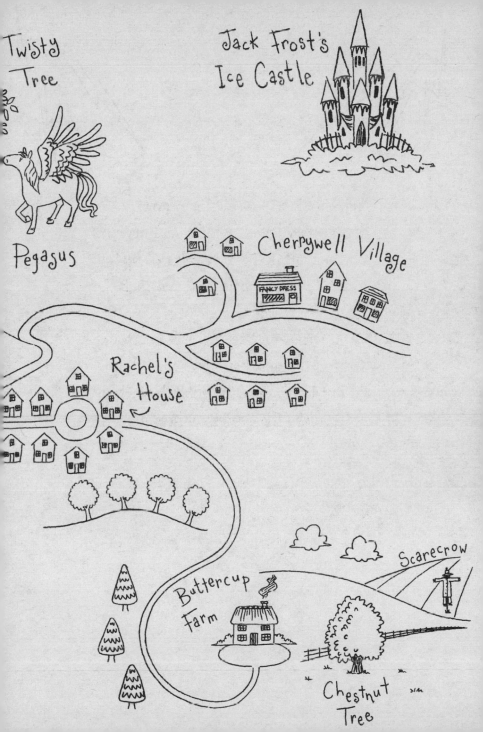

By frosty magic I cast away
These seven jewels with their fiery rays,
So their magic powers will not be felt
And my icy castle shall not melt.

The fairies may search high and low
To find the gems and take them home.
But I will send my goblin guards
To make the fairies' mission hard.

Contents

Goblins in Disguise

"There's a cool costume store!" Kirsty
Tate said, pointing at one of the shops on
Cherrywell's busy main street.

"Fun!" Rachel Walker replied happily.
"Let's go pick out costumes for Isabel's
Halloween party before the bus comes."

"OK," Kirsty agreed. She was staying
at Rachel's house for the week, and the

girls had just gone bowling with some of Rachel's friends from school. One of them, Isabel, had invited everyone to a Halloween party over the weekend.

"What do you want to dress up as?" Kirsty asked Rachel.

"Something magical, of course!" Rachel replied with a grin.

Kirsty smiled back. She and Rachel loved magic. It was because they shared an amazing secret: They were friends with the fairies!

Their magical adventures had all started one summer. The girls had helped the fairies stop mean Jack Frost from taking the color out of Fairyland. Since then, the Fairy King and Queen had asked for their help again and again. In fact, Rachel and Kirsty were right in the middle of another fairy adventure. Jack Frost was still causing trouble!

This time, he'd stolen seven sparkling jewels from Queen Titania's crown. The jewels were very special because they controlled important fairy powers, like the ability to fly, or to give children in the human world sweet dreams. Every year, in a special celebration, the fairies recharged their wands with the jewels' magic. This year's ceremony was just around the corner. If the jewels weren't found by then, the fairies would run out of their special magic completely!

Jack Frost had hoped to keep the magic jewels for himself. But when their magic had started to melt his ice castle, he had gotten very angry. He cast a spell to throw the gems far into the human world. Then he sent his mean goblins to guard them, so the fairies couldn't get them back.

Rachel and Kirsty had already helped three of the Jewel Fairies track down their magic gems. But there were still four jewels left to find!

"Do you think we'll find another jewel today?" Rachel whispered as she and Kirsty ran up to the store.

"I hope so," Kirsty replied.

A small boy and his mom were looking

at the display in the store window.
There were colorful lanterns and two
mannequins wearing Halloween costumes.
One was dressed as a witch, and the
other as a goblin.

Suddenly, the boy gasped. "Mom! Did
you see that?" he cried. "That goblin
costume just moved!"

Rachel and Kirsty stopped and glanced
at each other.

"Don't be silly, Tom." The boy's mom laughed, leading him away. "It's time to go!"

"A goblin mannequin that moves?" Kirsty hissed to Rachel. "We'd better take a look."

The girls peered closely at the window display. The mannequin the boy had pointed out was wearing a green goblin costume and a little red hat. Rachel's eyes widened as she took in the goblin's beady eyes, long nose, and great big feet.

"That's not a goblin costume!" she exclaimed. "It's a *real* goblin!"

"And look at the witch," Kirsty added. The witch mannequin wore a long black skirt and a pointed hat, and held a broomstick. Its lumpy green nose and warty chin looked awfully goblinlike, though.

"The witch is a goblin, too!" Rachel gasped.

Kirsty grabbed Rachel's arm. "Oh, Rachel, if there are goblins in the window, maybe one of the fairies' magic jewels is inside the store!"

Looking Out for Magic

"Let's go take a look!" Rachel cried. The girls pushed the door open and hurried down three stone steps into the store. A salesperson came rushing over to meet them. She had curly brown hair and a cheerful smile. "Hello," she said, stepping around a large pile of pumpkin buckets near the door. "May I help you?"

Rachel could feel her heart pounding.
"Um . . ." she began uncertainly. It
was hard to concentrate, knowing that
two goblins were standing just a few
feet away.

"Could we look at some costumes,
please?" Kirsty asked quickly. "We're
going to a Halloween party over the
weekend, and we don't have anything
to wear."

The salesperson smiled. "Well, you've come to the right place! My name's Maggie. I'm sure I can find something for the two of you. What did you have in mind?"

Kirsty looked around and spotted a display of cat costumes. "I think I'd like to try a cat costume, please," she said.

"Well, we have lots of choices," Maggie replied. She turned to Rachel. "How about you, my dear?"

Rachel thought fast. They needed to search the store for the magic jewel. If Kirsty could keep Maggie busy, then maybe Rachel could look around. "I haven't quite decided yet," she replied truthfully. "Would it be OK if I look around a little bit?"

"Of course," Maggie answered. She smiled at Kirsty. "Now, why don't you come with me to the dressing room, and I'll find a cat costume in your size?"

As Kirsty headed off with Maggie,

Rachel glanced around the store. There were racks of costumes, and shelves piled high with wigs, makeup, and masks. Rachel noticed a container full of plastic swords and a stand packed with fairy wings and wands. *If there is a magic jewel in this store*, she thought, *it could be anywhere!*

Her eyes fell on a pirate display near

the back of the store. There were two mannequins dressed in pirate costumes.

They stood on a fake desert island, and each pirate had an eye patch. Between them was a palm tree and a huge treasure chest with gold chains and strings of pearls spilling from it. *That would be the perfect place to hide a jewel*, Rachel thought.

As she drew closer to the treasure chest, her heart seemed to skip a beat. The chest was glowing with a deep golden light. *Magic!* Rachel thought, looking at the way the gold chains glittered and gleamed. *It has to be!* Holding her breath, she lifted the heavy lid of the chest.

Suddenly, a fountain of orange-and-gold sparkles shot into the air. Rachel gasped and nearly dropped the lid. Twirling in the middle of the sparkles was a tiny fairy!

Costumes Galore!

"Hello!" called the fairy brightly. She
was wearing a frilly yellow skirt, an
orange wraparound top, and sparkling
orange shoes. Her wavy black hair was
held back by a red headband.

"Hi!" Rachel replied in delight. She
thought she recognized the fairy. "Aren't
you Chloe the Topaz Fairy?"

Chloe nodded. "Yes, I am."

Rachel glanced back over her shoulder. Luckily, Maggie was busy handing clothes to Kirsty. She hadn't noticed the fairy. Rachel led Chloe behind a costume rack. "Is your topaz in this store?" she asked. "Kirsty and I thought it seemed like a magic jewel was nearby."

"The magic topaz is definitely in here. I can feel it," Chloe responded, perching on Rachel's hand. "But I haven't been able to find it. I was searching through the treasure chest when the lid shut. I was trapped inside! Thanks for rescuing me."

"No problem," Rachel said with a smile. She peeked around the side of the costume rack. "Have you seen the goblins?"

Chloe looked alarmed. "Goblins! What goblins?"

"There are two goblins in the window display. They're pretending to be mannequins," Rachel explained.

Chloe shivered. "They must be here to guard the topaz. We'll have to try to send it back to Fairyland without the goblins noticing."

"Yes," Rachel agreed. "But we need to find it first. Where should we look?" Just then, she heard the dressing room door open. She peeked around the clothing rack to see how Kirsty was doing. "The cat costume fits you just fine," Maggie was saying to Kirsty. "But you need some cat ears! Wait there, and I'll get you some from the stockroom."

When Maggie walked away, Rachel
hurried over to her friend.
"Kirsty!" she hissed.

"What is it?" Kirsty
asked eagerly. "Did you
find something? Oh!"
She gasped when she
saw Chloe fluttering
beside Rachel.

The little fairy grinned.
"Hi, I'm Chloe," she said.

"Chloe's topaz is somewhere
in this store," Rachel told Kirsty quietly.
"We have to find it!"

"What does it look like?" Kirsty asked.

"It's a deep golden color," Chloe
replied. "And it controls changing magic,
so keep your eyes open for any strange
changes."

"It might be hidden with those fairy wands," Rachel suggested, pointing to a display near by. "Let's check there."

"You do that, and I'll check the queen costume," Kirsty said, pointing to an outfit near the

window. It was a beautiful jeweled dress and cape with a crown of glittering gems. "The topaz could easily hide there." Just then, Rachel's sharp ears caught the sound of footsteps.

"Maggie's coming back!" she warned.
She and Chloe slipped behind the
costume rack again.

"Let's check the fairy wand display,"
Rachel whispered to Chloe. "If you hide
in the pocket of my coat, Maggie won't
be able to see you."

Chloe dived into Rachel's pocket, and
they headed over to look at the wands.

Meanwhile, Maggie handed Kirsty a pair of cat ears.

"Um," Kirsty began. "I'm really sorry, but I just noticed that queen costume. It's so beautiful! Would you mind if I tried that one on, instead?"

"Of course not!" Maggie replied cheerfully. "I'll go get it for you." She bustled over to the store window and took the costume off the mannequin. "Here we are!" she said, heading back to Kirsty with the costume in her arms.

As Maggie carried the costume past the

window, Kirsty heard a faint *pop*. The air behind Maggie shimmered with a golden glow. Then, to Kirsty's amazement, the witch costume on the goblin in the window changed into a suit of armor! Kirsty gasped and looked around quickly for her friends. She was sure that the costume change was the work of Chloe's magic topaz!

Lots of Changes

Maggie walked closer to Kirsty. Behind her, the goblins in the window looked around in confusion. The metal visor on the suit of armor fell down with a dull clunk, and the goblin inside let out a muffled shriek of surprise.

Hearing the noise, Maggie turned around. She stared at the suit of armor.

"Where did that come from?" she murmured. "I thought there was a witch costume in the window." She turned back to Kirsty. "Did you see a witch costume?"

Kirsty didn't know what to say. "Um, I can't really remember," she replied.

"Maybe someone changed the costumes yesterday. That was my day off," Maggie explained. "But I'm surprised I didn't notice earlier!"

Behind Maggie, Kirsty could see the goblin in the red hat smirking at his friend, who was struggling to yank open the heavy visor of his helmet.

Meanwhile, Maggie was shaking out the queen costume so that Kirsty could try it on. As she did, there was another faint *pop*. Kirsty looked around nervously. This time, she saw the air shimmer with a red glow. Then the bow and arrows on a nearby Robin Hood costume turned into a set of bagpipes!

Kirsty's hand flew to her mouth. She hoped Maggie wouldn't notice the change. She had no idea how to explain why Robin Hood was now holding bagpipes!

She bit her lip as the earrings on a display to Maggie's left suddenly turned into pink-and-white striped candy. *The topaz must be inside something that Maggie is holding!* Kirsty thought.

Suddenly, she saw the goblin in armor step cautiously out of the window display. He had his visor open now, and his beady eyes were fixed on the costume in Maggie's arms. *Oh, no!* Kirsty thought. *The goblin must have seen the magic working, too.*

She watched anxiously as the goblin inched slowly toward Maggie. But, as he did, one of his big feet bumped into a container of plastic swords. The rattle made Maggie turn around.

Grabbing a sword, the goblin froze as if he was just another store display!

"Thanks for the costume," Kirsty said quickly, trying to distract Maggie. "Can I try it on now?"

Maggie looked at the suit of armor, puzzled, and turned back to Kirsty. "Of course," she replied. She helped Kirsty into the dress and draped the cape over her shoulders.

As Kirsty took the crown, she noticed a huge golden stone in the middle of it. The stone seemed to shimmer and shine. Could it be the magic topaz? Kirsty put on the crown. Immediately, her head started to

tingle with fairy magic. "Oh, wow!" she
breathed.

"Do you like it?" Maggie smiled. "I
think I have a scepter in the stockroom
that would look great with that costume.
I'll see if I can find it for you."

As soon as Maggie had left, Kirsty
looked for Rachel and Chloe behind the
fairy display. "I have the topaz!" she
called softly.

"Hooray!" Rachel
exclaimed.

"Where is it?"
asked Chloe,
zooming out of
Rachel's pocket in
a whoosh of sparks.

"In the crown on
my head!" replied Kirsty.

Rachel looked at Kirsty's head in surprise. "Crown?" she asked. "Do you mean the turban?"

Kirsty turned to look in the dressing room mirror. Immediately, she saw that the crown had changed into a turban! The golden topaz still glittered at its center. "It changed!" she breathed.

At that moment, Rachel let out a cry of alarm. "Kirsty!"

"Watch out!" Chloe exclaimed at the same time.

Kirsty whirled around to see that the goblin in armor had crept up on her while she wasn't looking. Cackling gleefully, he leaped forward and snatched the turban with the topaz right off Kirsty's head!

Stop That Goblin!

"I have the topaz!" the goblin shouted.
He staggered through the store with the
turban and its precious, glowing jewel.

"After him!" Kirsty cried. The goblin
charged toward the entrance door, his
metal armor clanking.

Rachel and Chloe raced after him.

"Come on!" the goblin in the red hat

shouted, running up the steps toward the door. But the armor wasn't easy for his friend to run in. The visor fell down over his eyes again, and he couldn't see anything! He bumped clumsily into the pile of Halloween buckets, sending them bouncing and rolling across the floor.

The goblin tripped over one of the buckets and lost his balance. "Whaaaa!" he cried, tumbling to the floor. As he fell,

the turban slipped from his hands and
flew through the air.

"You klutz!" the other goblin sputtered.
"What do you think you're doing?"

"I can't see," the armored goblin
whined, trying to pull his visor up. "And
now I've hurt myself!"

"Catch that turban, Rachel!" Kirsty
exclaimed as the turban flew through
the air.

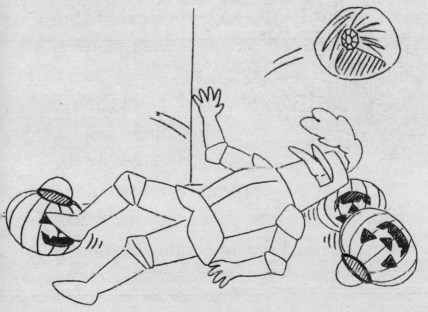

Rachel reached for it, but missed. As the turban hit the ground, the topaz was jolted out of its setting. The golden gem bounced across the floor and rolled in among the scattered buckets.

There was a loud *pop* and a shimmer of golden light. In the blink of an eye, all the pumpkins had changed into pineapples!

"Where's the topaz?" Kirsty cried, running over.

"I can see it!" Chloe gasped, swooping toward the pineapples and pointing with her wand.

Kirsty spotted the topaz glowing among

the fruit, too. But as Chloe zoomed
down to grab it,
the goblin by the
door also
spotted it.
He slid
through the
pineapples
as if he was
on ice and
scooped the
topaz up with
one hand just
before Chloe
reached it.

   "Ow!" he
wailed as the heat
of the magic jewel
burned his icy goblin skin.

For a moment, Kirsty felt a glimmer of hope. She remembered that goblins couldn't touch the magic jewels with their bare hands. The jewels' magic burned them! She waited for the goblin to drop the topaz.

But instead, there was another loud *pop*. The goblin's costume and hat changed into a teddy-bear costume, complete with furry gloves that looked like paws!

"I have the topaz!" the teddy-bear goblin shouted triumphantly to his friend, who was scrambling out of his metal armor. "Let's go!" Clutching the jewel in his furry paws, he charged toward the door.

Chloe swooped at the teddy-bear goblin's head. "Give me back my jewel!" she cried.

"No!" the goblin shouted. "The topaz isn't yours anymore. It's ours, and you're never going to get it back!"

"Come on, Kirsty!" Rachel cried. "We have to stop them!"

She and Kirsty began to run through the pineapples, trying not to trip. The goblins had reached the steps. They were going to get away with the topaz! But then, suddenly, Rachel had an idea. She picked up a pineapple as if it was a bowling ball. With a thrust of her arm, she sent it rolling across the floor — right at the two goblins.

The pineapple hit the feet of the goblin who had been dressed in armor. He yelped in surprise and grabbed the arm of the teddy-bear goblin, who was halfway up the steps. For a moment, both goblins teetered on the steps, arms flailing. Then they toppled down the stairs and landed in a heap.

The topaz flew out of the goblin's furry paw and went spinning through the air. As it sailed past the lights, there was another *pop*. The air shimmered with an amber glow, and suddenly all the store lights became tiny disco balls that sparkled with magic.

Chloe raced after the jewel, and caught it in both hands. But it was too heavy for her to fly with. "Whoa!" she cried in alarm, her wings fluttering frantically. She and the jewel sank quickly toward the ground.

"Help!" Kirsty scrambled to her feet and dived for the fairy with her hands outstretched. Chloe and the Topaz both landed safely in her palms. Kirsty pulled her hands to her chest, her heart beating fast. Was Chloe OK?

"Phew!" Chloe said, poking her head out of Kirsty's cupped hands and grinning.

"That was close. Thanks for catching me, Kirsty!"

"Are you all right?" Rachel asked, scrambling over and looking down at the fairy in concern.

"I'm fine," Chloe replied. Her hair was standing on end, but her brown eyes were sparkling. "In fact, I'm better than fine," she said, looking at the groaning goblins. "I have my topaz back!"

Just then, there was a noise from the stockroom. "I found the scepter!" Maggie called cheerfully. "I'll be out in a minute, once I put these boxes away."

"Oh, no!" Rachel gasped. "I forgot about Maggie." She looked around the store. There were pineapples all over the floor, glittering disco balls instead of lights, and pieces of armor scattered everywhere. Plus, the window display was ruined because its two mannequins were tangled in a heap by the door!

"Maggie will be really upset about this mess!" Kirsty said.

"Don't worry," Chloe replied cheerfully. "Now that I have the topaz back, I can work some changing magic." She touched her golden wand to the topaz in Kirsty's hand.

The tip of the wand began to gleam like a sparkling ray of sunshine. The little fairy lifted it high in the air and waved it expertly.

There was a quick series of *pops*, and everything started to change again. The air glimmered orange, then red, and finally gold. Then pineapples changed back to pumpkin buckets, the disco balls changed to normal lights, and two normal mannequins appeared in the window. Everything was magically back to how it had been in the first place! With a final *pop*, all the pieces of armor jumped neatly onto a shelf.

"Phew!" Rachel said in relief.

Chloe smiled at her. "It's all back to normal."

"Except for one thing," Kirsty said slowly. "What's Maggie going to say when she sees those goblins?"

Fluffy Bunnies

The goblins were picking themselves up off the floor, groaning and arguing. Their costumes had disappeared and they were back to their ordinary green goblin selves.

"Why did you trip me like that?" the first goblin demanded.

"Why did you let go of the topaz?"

sputtered the other. "This is all your fault!"

"My fault? It's *your* fault!" the first goblin shouted.

"Oh, no. How are we going to explain those two to Maggie?" Rachel asked.

"Leave it to me!" Chloe flew over to the goblins.

"Pesky fairy!" snarled the first goblin, making a swipe at Chloe, who darted easily out of his way. "Give us back that topaz!"

"No," Chloe replied coolly. "And my wand is charged with changing magic now, so I can turn you

into anything I want!" She smiled. "If
you don't leave the store this minute, I'm
going to turn you both into fluffy pink
bunny rabbits!"

The goblins' mouths dropped open in
horror.

"Bunny rabbits!" the first one
exclaimed. "Yuck!"

"You wouldn't!" said the second.

Chloe grinned. "Oh, yes I would." She
gave Rachel and Kirsty a mischievous
look. "What do you two think?"

Rachel grinned back. "I think they'd make cute bunny rabbits," she said.

"Especially fluffy pink ones," Kirsty added.

Chloe lifted her wand.

"Noooooo!" both goblins cried in alarm. They turned and ran up the steps. Pushing and shoving, they yanked the door open and disappeared down the street as fast as they could run.

Rachel, Kirsty, and Chloe all burst out laughing.

"You girls seem to be having a good time," Maggie said, stepping out of the stockroom with a scepter in her hand.

Chloe darted into Rachel's pocket just in time.

"I'm sorry I took so long," Maggie added. She looked at the door, which was just swinging shut. "Have I missed a customer?"

"It's OK," said Kirsty, quickly putting the topaz back in her pocket. "It was just, er . . ."

"Someone looking for pineapples," Rachel finished quickly.

Kirsty hid a grin while Maggie looked at Rachel in surprise. "Pineapples?" she asked.

Rachel nodded. "When they realized you didn't sell any, they left," she added.

"Oh, how strange." Maggie blinked. "Well, never mind. Here's the scepter," she said, handing it to Kirsty. She turned

to Rachel. "Have you decided on your
costume yet?"

"I think I'd liked to dress up as a fairy,"
Rachel replied. "You have some
beautiful fairy wings and wands."

"Yes," Kirsty agreed, handing the
scepter back to Maggie.
"Thank you for letting
me try on the costumes,
but I think I'd like to
dress up as a fairy,
too." She saw
Chloe's head pop
out of Rachel's
pocket. The fairy grinned
and gave her a thumbs-up sign
before quickly ducking back down.

Kirsty changed out of the queen
costume and the girls each chose a pair

of wings and a wand. Just as they finished paying for them, the phone rang. "Enjoy your Halloween party, girls!" Maggie said as she hurried off to answer the call.

The moment she disappeared, Chloe flew out of Rachel's pocket in a cloud of fairy dust. "I wish I could stay for your party. I bet you'll look great in your fairy costumes! But I'd better get back to Fairyland now. Thank you for helping me find the topaz." Kirsty took the stone out of her pocket.

"Here it is," she said holding it out to the fairy.

Chloe touched her wand to the golden jewel. It disappeared safely back to Fairyland in a fountain of orange sparkles.

Rachel and Kirsty picked up their

shopping bags and headed out of
the shop.

"See you soon!" Chloe said as Rachel
pulled the door open.

"Bye!" the girls called. The little fairy
spun around in a swirl of golden light,
and then zoomed away.

"I'm so glad we were able to help her," Rachel said happily.

"Me, too," Kirsty agreed. A sparkle near the ceiling caught her eye, and she looked up. A single tiny disco ball was still hanging there, glittering and shining with fairy magic. "Look!" she exclaimed. "Chloe left one little disco ball behind."

Rachel laughed. "There will always be magic in the store now," she said. Then she spotted the bus turning onto Main Street. "Come on!" she gasped, pulling the door closed behind them. "We have to catch the bus, Kirsty!"

They began to run down the street. "It's been an amazing day, hasn't it?"

Kirsty panted. "What do you think will happen tomorrow?"

"I don't know," Rachel said, as they reached the bus stop just in time and jumped on board the bus. She grinned at Kirsty. "But I bet it will be magical!"

The Jewel Fairies

Rachel and Kirsty have helped India,
Scarlett, Emily, and Chloe all
get their jewels back. Can they help

Amy the
Amethyst Fairy,

too?

Ready for Adventure

"Kirsty, we're here!" Rachel Walker announced, looking out of the car window. She pointed at a large sign that read WELCOME TO TIPPINGTON MANOR.

Kirsty Tate, Rachel's best friend, was peering up at the cloudy sky. "I hope it doesn't rain," she said. Then the house caught her eye. "Oh, look, Rachel, there's the house! Isn't it beautiful?"

At the bottom of the long, sweeping gravel driveway stood Tippington Manor. It was a huge Victorian house with an enormous wooden door, rows of tall windows, and ivy climbing all over its old red bricks. The house was surrounded by gardens full of flowers and trees, their autumn leaves glowing in shades of red and gold.

"Look over there, Kirsty," Rachel said to her friend as Mr. Walker turned the car into the parking lot. "The Adventure Playground!"

Kirsty looked to where Rachel was pointing. She was excited to see the playground on a hill behind the house.

She glimpsed some tires dangling on ropes, a silver slide, and what looked like a big wooden treehouse in the center, built around a towering oak tree.

"Isn't it great?" Kirsty whispered to Rachel as they climbed out of the car. "The fairies would *love* that treehouse!"

Rachel grinned and nodded. She and Kirsty were lucky enough to be friends with the fairies! Whenever there was trouble in Fairyland, the two girls helped the fairies any way they could. They had already had lots of magical adventures, and they were sure there were more to come!

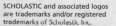
 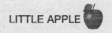

A fairy for every day!

The seven Rainbow Fairies are missing! Help rescue the fairies and bring the sparkle back to Fairyland.

When mean Jack Frost steals the Weather Fairies' magical feathers, the weather turns wacky. It's up to the Weather Fairies to fix it!

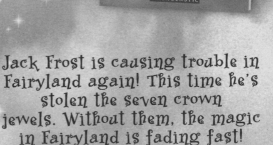

Jack Frost is causing trouble in Fairyland again! This time he's stolen the seven crown jewels. Without them, the magic in Fairyland is fading fast!

Look for The Pet Fairies— Coming soon!

■ SCHOLASTIC
www.scholastic.com

FAIRY